counting
comic
history puzzle
electronic craft sticker
spot-the-difference
scary
picture

This book belongs to

BEN, Bella, and...

_____

_____

For Gail and for Friendly, her fondly remembered dog

Henry Holt and Company, LLC
Publishers since 1866
175 Fifth Avenue
New York, New York 10010
mackids.com

Library of Congress Cataloging-in-Publication Data

Byrne, Richard, 1963– author, illustrator.
We're in the wrong book! / Richard Byrne.—First American edition.
pages   cm
Summary: When Bella's dog bumps Bella and Ben off the page,
they land in the wrong book.
ISBN 978-1-62779-451-0 (hardcover)
[1. Books and reading—Fiction. 2. Humorous stories.] I. Title.
II. Title: We are in the wrong book!
PZ7.B9962We 2015   [E]—dc23   2015003704

Henry Holt books may be purchased for business or promotional use.
For information on bulk purchases, please contact the Macmillan
Corporate and Premium Sales Department at (800) 221-7945 x5442
or by e-mail at specialmarkets@macmillan.com.

First published in hardcover in 2015 by Oxford University Press
First American edition—2015
Printed in China by Leo Paper Group, Gulao Town, Heshan,
Guangdong Province

10 9 8 7 6 5 4 3 2 1

We're in the wrong book!

Richard BYRNE

Henry Holt and Company · New York

Bella and Ben were jumping down the street, from one side of the book . . .

to the other.

Then Bella's dog joined in . . .

"Where's my dog?" said Bella.

9 Pencils

"Where
are we?"
said Ben.

10 Lollipops

"We're in the wrong book!"

9 Pencils

"Well, let's jump back into
the right book," said Ben.

But they jumped into . . . .

10 Lollipops

. . . somebody else's COMIC book!

Yikes!

Eeek!

"We're trying to get back to our own book," explained Ben and Bella.

"We know someone who can help," said Mouse. "Follow us."

Ben and Bella described their book to the lovely librarian.

"It has tall buildings . . ."

". . . and an enormous dog."

"I know the book," she said.

"It's through there."

HISTORY BOOKS

"I hope she's right," said Bella.

"What does it all mean?" asked Ben.

"I think it says 'Walk this way,'" said Bella.

But things just got more and more puzzling.

And when Bella thought she had found a path that would lead them back to their book . . .

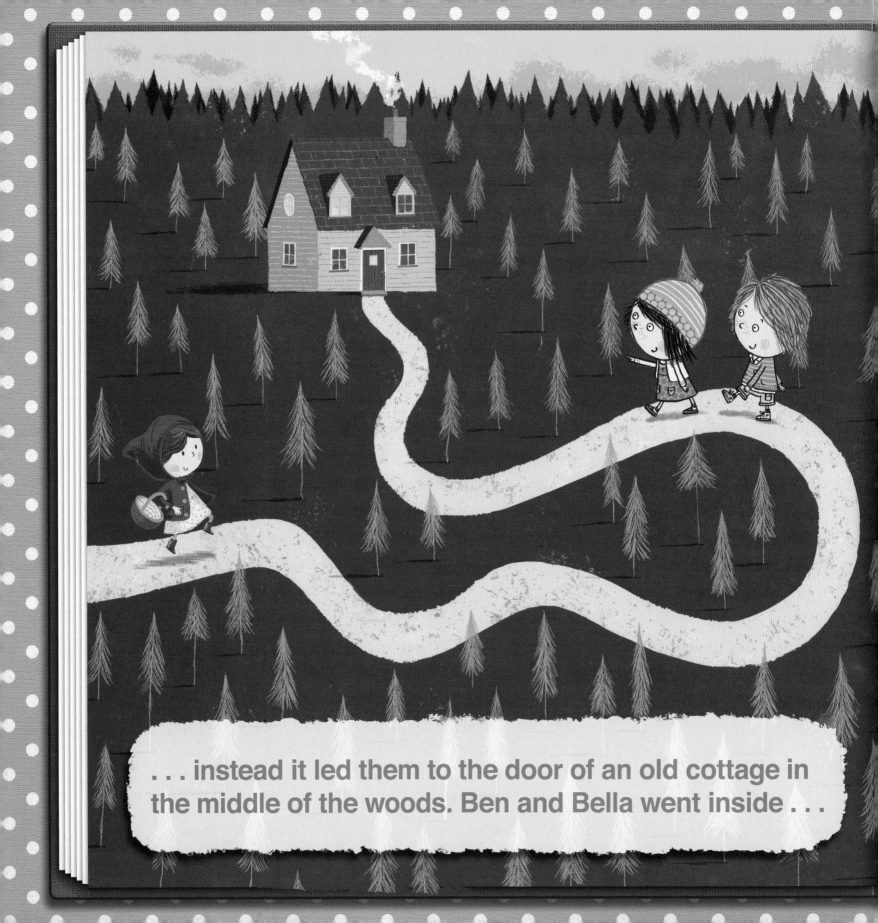

. . . instead it led them to the door of an old cottage in the middle of the woods. Ben and Bella went inside . . .

where an odd-looking lady invited them to stay for dinner. "Thank you, but we really must get back to our own book," said Bella. Ben thought he could see a way back.

Suddenly, Ben and Bella were in a book full of instructions. "I suppose we could follow them," said Bella.

1 Take a piece of rectangular paper.

It doesn't have to be this huge!

2 Fold it in half.

3 Fold a top corner toward the center.

4 Fold the other corner.

5 Fold up the flap at the bottom.

6 Turn over and repeat.

7 Fold both corners of the flap inward.

8 Turn over and repeat.

9 Hold the bottom-center fold of each side and pull outward.

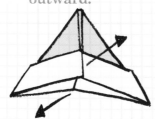

10 Press flat.

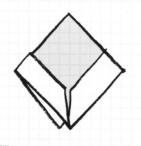

11 Fold the bottom triangle up.

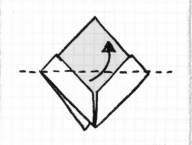

12 Turn over and repeat.

13 Hold the bottom-center fold of each side and pull outward. Press flat.

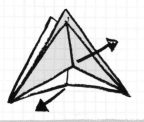

14 Hold the top-outer corners and pull outward.

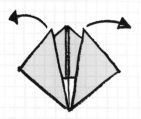

15 Your boat is ready to sail!

"Book ahoy!" said Ben.

"The WRONG book ahoy!" grumbled Bella. "And now we're stuck in it!"

So they stuck themselves in a hot-air balloon as it lifted up, up, and away.

The balloon landed in just the right spot . . .

Can you spot ten differences between these two pictures?

for spotting a very helpful sign.

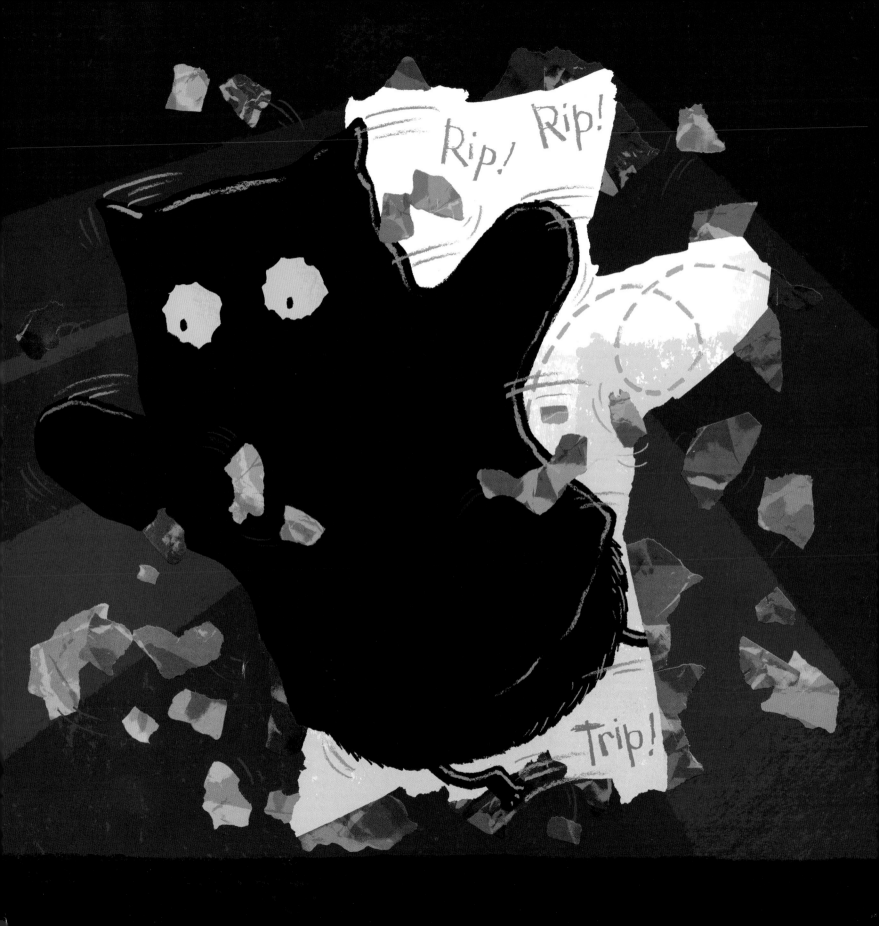

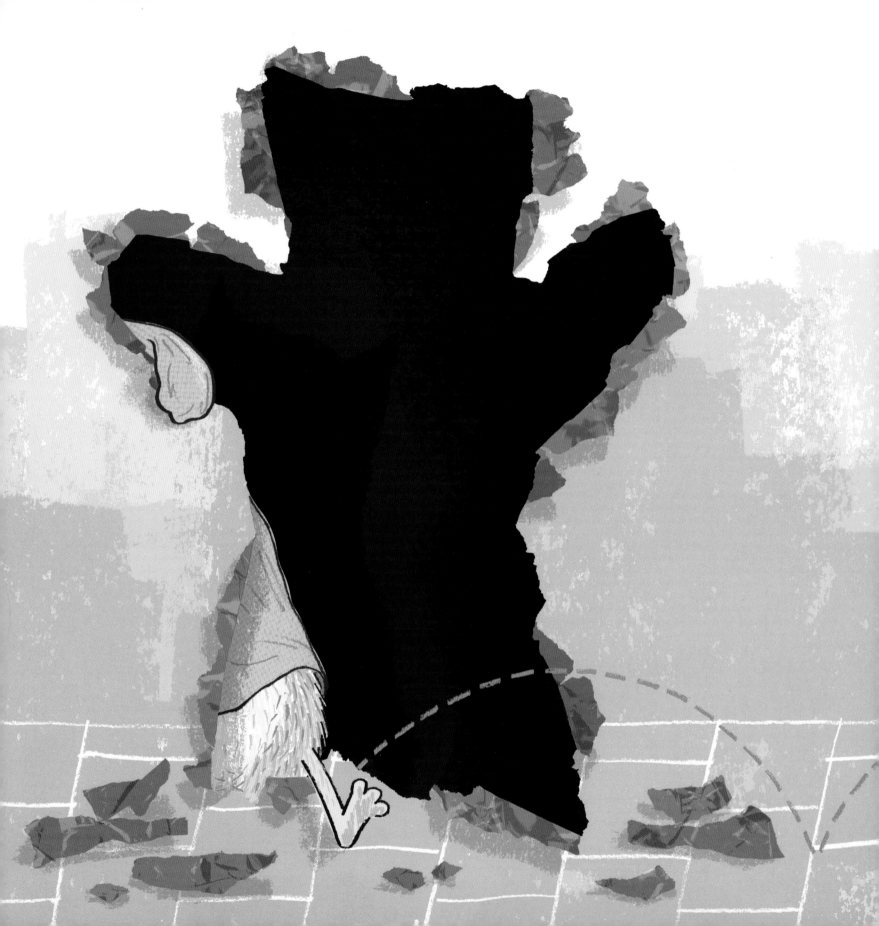

And they both jumped through
the monster-shaped hole.

"Yay!" said Bella.
"We're back in our book!"

When Ben and Bella came back to fix the hole in their book, there was no sign of the monster.

"Thank goodness!" said Bella. "Now, where's my dog?"